Whispers in the Shadows

A SUSPENSEFUL JOURNEY INTO THE HEART OF DECEIT

YASHWANTH KANTAMSETTY

BlueRoseONE.com
Stories Matter
NewDelhi • London

BLUEROSE PUBLISHERS
India | U.K.

For permissions requests or inquiries regarding this publication, please contact:

BLUEROSE PUBLISHERS
www.BlueRoseONE.com
info@bluerosepublishers.com
+91 8882 898 898
+4407342408967

ISBN: 978-93-7310-010-4

First Edition: September 2025

We were never wrong for each other
just right at the wrong time,
and time never forgives..

Love

Vs

Time

I still remember when you smiled at me,
Like the sun breaking through the darkest sea.
Your laugh was my favorite melody,
Now silence echoes where your voice used to be.
I keep looking for you in the places we used to go,
But the rooms feel empty, and the lights are dim and.
cold.
If I could turn back time, just to hold you once again,
I would cross all the skies, just to feel your love again
where are you?
My heart is lost without you,
The world feels so far away,
And I can't seem to find my way.
I still need you,
You're the dream I can't undo,
I search for you, in every star,
But you're gone, and I'm here, so far.
I still need you,
You're the dream I can't undo,
I search for you, in every star,
But you're gone, and I'm here, so far
"The daughter of caleb" where are you?
In my heart, you'll stay true,
Even when the world fades away,
I'll keep loving you, every single day...

Let's read how time play in our lives and relationships...

THE COLD STRANGERS

GENRE

Romance / Tragedy

DRAMA

Slow-burn Psychological Fiction
(Subtle Speculative Element – Time perception in isolation)

Theme

A story of two lost souls who meet in the most isolated, frozen place on Earth. In a land where time stretches and reality blurs, they find a fleeting warmth in each other. But time, distance, and the world beyond the snow eventually pull them apart. It's about how love can bloom even in the coldest, darkest places and how time doesn't always move forward the same for everyone.

The biting wind, a relentless sculptor, carved icicles from the eaves of the old lodge, each one a crystalline dagger. My breath plumed white, a ghostly whisper in the frigid air, as I huddled deeper into my worn wool coat. The sky, a bruised canvas of grey, wept. Not tears, but a deluge of icy rain, each drop a tiny hammer blow against the frozen ground. I'd been caught, utterly unprepared, miles from anywhere, my car a sputtering, pathetic heap back on the treacherous mountain pass

Well, isn't this just delightful," I muttered, pulling my scarf higher, the wool rough against my chin. "A proper winter wonderland, if your idea of wonder involves frostbite and hypothermia

Asudden gust ripped through the valley, rattling the ancient windowpanes of the lodge. I ducked my head, shivering. The rain intensified, a solid sheet of water cascading from the heavens. That's when I saw her. A figure, silhouetted against the stormy sky, running, not walking, across the snow-dusted lawn. She wore only a thin, dark dress, her hair, a cascade of midnight, plastered to her face. She looked like a drowned raven, beautiful and utterly out of place in this desolate, icy landscape.....

She stumbled, a small gasp escaping her lips, and then she was at the lodge door, pushing it open with a desperate shove. The wind howled, a hungry beast, as she slipped inside, dripping water onto the polished wooden floor. Her eyes, wide and startled, met mine. They were the color of deep forest moss after a summer rain, framed by long, dark lashes.

Oh, my God," she whispered, her voice a fragile thing against the storm's roar. "I didn't think anyone was here."

"Just me," I replied, my voice rougher than I intended. "And this delightful weather. Are you alright? You're soaked."

She shivered violently, her arms wrapping around herself. "I... I ran out. I just needed to run."

From what?" I asked, stepping closer, my gaze tracing the rivulets of water on her cheeks. They mingled with what looked suspiciously like tear tracks.

"Everything," she choked out, a raw, wounded sound. "Just... everything."

I hesitated, then stripped off my own coat. "Here. You'll freeze."

Her eyes widened, a flicker of surprise in their depths. "No, I couldn't possibly. You need it."

"I'm already half-frozen," I said, trying for a light tone. "One more layer won't make a difference. You, on the other hand, look like you just swam the Arctic Ocean." I held it out.

She looked at the coat, then at me, a tiny, almost imperceptible nod. "Thank you," she murmured, her voice barely a breath. She took the coat, its warmth a stark contrast to her icy skin, and pulled it around her, burying her face in the collar. The faint scent of pine and something uniquely *me* seemed to calm her.

I'm Elias," I offered, extending a hand. She looked up, a small, tentative smile gracing her lips. "Lila." Her hand, surprisingly delicate, slipped into mine. Her fingers were like ice.

Lila," I repeated, the name a soft melody on my tongue. "It's good to meet you, Lila. Even if it is under such... soggy circumstances."

She actually laughed then, a low, melodic sound that chased away some of the storm's chill. "You could say that. I think I just ran through a waterfall."

"Well, at least you have a story to tell. And now, you have a warm coat. Come on, there's a fireplace over here. We can try to dry off."

We spent the next few hours by the roaring fire, the only sounds the crackle of burning logs and the relentless drumming of rain against the windows. We talked, hesitant at first, then with a growing ease that surprised us both. She told me about her life, a whirlwind of expectations and pressures that had driven her to this remote lodge, seeking a moment of peace. I told her about my own nomadic existence, chasing stories and landscapes with my camera.

It's beautiful here, isn't it?" she said, gazing into the flames, her face illuminated by the dancing light. "Even with the storm."

"It has a certain wild charm," I agreed, watching the firelight play in her hair. "Like you."

She turned, her eyes meeting mine, and a blush crept up her neck. "And you, Elias. You're... an unexpected kindness."

"Perhaps we were both meant to be caught in this storm," I said, my voice dropping, "to find shelter here, together."

A long silence stretched between us, filled only by the rhythmic *thump-thump* of the rain. The air was thick with unspoken possibility.

"I think I'd like that," she finally whispered, her eyes still locked on mine.

That night, the storm raged outside, but inside, a different kind of warmth bloomed. We shared stories, shared laughter, and as the hours melted away, we shared a kiss, tentative at first, then deep and consuming, a promise whispered against the roar of the wind.

The next morning, the world was transformed. Everything was blanketed in a pristine layer of snow, sparkling under a pale, winter sun. The air was crisp, clean, and impossibly quiet. My car was still out of

commission, but suddenly, it didn't matter.

Look," she breathed, her hand slipping into mine as we stood by the window, gazing out at the snow-covered peaks. "It's a different world."

"It is," I agreed, squeezing her hand. "And I don't want to leave it."

She turned, her smile radiant. "Then don't. Not yet."

We stayed. Days bled into weeks, weeks into months. The lodge, once a temporary refuge, became our world. We hiked through snow-laden forests, built snowmen with crooked smiles, and carved our initials into the frosted windowpanes. We cooked together, laughed until our sides ached, and fell asleep tangled in each other's arms, the scent of pine and woodsmoke clinging to our skin.

Elias," she'd hum, nestled against my chest, "do you ever think about how we met? Just two strangers, caught in a storm."

"Every day," I'd murmur, kissing the top of her

head. "It feels like a dream, doesn't it? This whole life we've built here."

"A beautiful dream," she'd sigh contentedly. "I never knew love could feel like this. So... complete."

I felt it too. A profound, soul-deep connection. She was the calm to my storm, the quiet melody to my restless heart. Our days were filled with an easy joy, a shared understanding that transcended words. We were two halves, finally made whole.

But even in our secluded paradise, the world outside eventually intruded. The first cracks were subtle, almost imperceptible. A phone call from her family, demanding her return. A missed deadline for my photography work. Small things, easily dismissed at first

It's just... my mother," she'd say, her voice tight, after a particularly long call. "She doesn't understand why I'm still here."

"She'll understand when she sees how happy you are," I'd reassure her, though a sliver of doubt had begun to lodge itself in my own heart.

Then, the disagreements started. Small at first, like pebbles in a shoe.

"You're always so focused on your work, Elias," she accused one evening, her voice sharp, after I'd spent hours editing photos instead of talking to her. "It's like I'm not even here sometimes."

"I'm trying to make a living, Lila," I retorted, my own patience wearing thin. "This isn't some endless vacation. We need money."

Money? Is that all you care about now? What happened to us? To just being together?"

The words hung in the air, cold and heavy. We'd never spoken to each other like that before. A silence descended, not comfortable, but strained, filled with a tension that hummed between us.

The pebbles turned into rocks. The outside pressures mounted. Her family's pleas became demands. My work became a relentless grind. The idyllic bubble we'd built began to deflate, slowly, agonizingly.

“You’re changing, Elias,” she cried one night, her voice trembling. “You’re not the man I met in the storm. You’re distant. You’re always on your phone, always thinking about something else.”

“And you, Lila!” I shot back, frustration boiling over. “You’re so consumed by your family’s expectations, you’re forgetting what we have! Don’t you think I feel it too? This... pressure?”

“Pressure? This is my life! My responsibilities!” she screamed, her voice cracking. “You just want to escape everything, don’t you? That’s why you’re here, hiding in this lodge!”

Hiding? I’m building a life! A life with you!” I roared, the words echoing off the wooden walls. “But it seems you’d rather go back to your gilded cage than fight for what we have!”

“Fight? Is that what this is now? A fight?” Her eyes, once so full of warmth, were now blazing with hurt and anger. “This isn’t love, Elias. This is... a battlefield.”

The arguments became more frequent, more

vicious. Words were thrown like daggers, each one leaving a fresh wound. The laughter faded, replaced by strained silences and bitter accusations. The lodge, once our sanctuary, felt like a prison. The biting cold outside seemed to seep into our very bones, chilling the love that had once burned so brightly.

One frigid morning, the sky a bleak, uncompromising grey, the air thick with unspoken words, she stood by the window, her back to me. The silence was deafening.

"I can't do this anymore, Elias," she said, her voice flat, devoid of emotion. It was worse than any scream.

My heart lurched, a cold stone in my chest. "What are you talking about, Lila?"

She turned, her face pale, her eyes haunted. "Us. This. It's... broken. We're just hurting each other."

"No," I whispered, stepping towards her, my hand reaching out. "Don't say that. We can fix this. We just need to... to try harder."

She flinched from my touch. "We've been trying, Elias. And all it does is make us miserable. We're not the same people we were when we met. The storm is over. And look what's left." She gestured vaguely at the desolate landscape outside.

"But I love you, Lila," I pleaded, the words torn from my throat. "I still love you." "I know," she said, and a single tear traced a path down her cheek. "And I love you too. But love isn't enough when it's like this. It's not fair to either of us. We're drowning in it."

"Please," I begged, my voice cracking. "Don't go. We can find a way. We have to."

There is no way," she replied, her voice barely audible. "Not anymore. We've changed. And the world outside... it's pulling us apart. It always was."

She walked to the door, her movements slow, deliberate. My chest ached, a hollow, gaping wound. I wanted to scream, to pull her back, to chain her to me, but I couldn't. The words were stuck, a lump of ice in my throat.

"Goodbye, Elias," she whispered, her voice a

ghost of its former self.

Then, she was gone. The door clicked shut, a final, definitive sound that echoed in the sudden, crushing silence. The lodge, once filled with our laughter and love, became a tomb. I stood there, frozen, watching the snow fall, each flake a tiny, cold memory. The storm had brought us together, and the calm had torn us apart.

Days blurred into weeks. The lodge became my solitary confinement. Every corner held a memory, every creak of the old wood a phantom whisper of her name. I saw her everywhere: her smile reflected in the frost on the window, her scent clinging to the old blanket on the sofa, her voice in the murmur of the wind. The silence was a constant, mocking companion. I couldn't eat, couldn't sleep.

My camera lay forgotten, gathering dust. The cold outside was nothing compared to the desolation within...

I tried to reach out. Countless calls, texts, voicemails. Each one unanswered. Each one a fresh stab of pain.

"Lila, please," I'd whisper into my phone, my voice raw and hoarse. "Just talk to me. I miss you. I miss us."

Nothing. Just the endless, soul-crushing silence.

One day, weeks later, a letter arrived. A crisp, white envelope, her handwriting elegant and unfamiliar. My hands trembled as I opened it...Elias,,

I know this is hard. Believe me, it's tearing me apart too. Every single day. I see you in everything. The snow, the cold, the way the light hits the mountains. It's a constant ache. I can't stop thinking about you, about us, about that first day in the storm. It was the most beautiful time of my life. You were the most beautiful part of my life...

Trying to forget the wild, beautiful, impossible dream we had...

*I still love you. God, I still love you so much it hurts to breathe. But some loves aren't meant to survive the real world. Some loves are meant to stay in the storm, where they were born, pure and

untainted...

Please, don't look for me. Don't try to find me. We both need to heal. And we can't do that if we keep picking at the wounds..

Goodbye, my Elias. Truly. Goodbye.

Lila..

The letter slipped from my numb fingers, fluttering to the floor like a dying bird. A ragged, guttural cry tore from my chest, a sound of pure, unadulterated agony. I sank to my knees, the cold wooden floor pressing against my skin, but I felt nothing. Only the crushing weight of her words, of her finality...

No!" I screamed, the sound echoing through the empty lodge, a desperate plea to a God who wasn't listening. "No! Lila, don't do this! Don't leave me!"

But she had. She was gone. And the vast, empty expanse of the world, once filled with the promise of our love, was now just a cold, silent testament to what we had lost. The storm had brought us together, but the quiet had pulled us apart. And time, that

relentless, indifferent force, had sealed our fate, ensuring that two souls, once intertwined by a twist of fate and a deluge of rain, would forever remain apart, bound only by the ghost of a love that was too beautiful, too fragile, to survive the harsh light of reality. I was left with the silence, the cold, and the relentless, heartbreaking echo of her name...

The Sky Knows Our Names

Some hearts beat in silence. Some stories whisper through the wind...

GENRE

Emotional Romance
Fate and Soul Connection
Time-Split Narrative / Magical Realism

Theme
Love Across Lifetimes
Destiny Written in the Sky
Memory and Time
Grief, Hope, and Rebirth
Eternal Connection Through Nature Somewhere,
far beyond the clouds,
two names are etched into the stars
names the world has forgotten
but the sky never did

I. The First Meeting – Rain and Notebooks

Aarav met Elira on a day that smelled like new rain and old books.

He had just moved into the sleepy hill town of Vaelon, transferring colleges after losing his brother in a car accident. He wanted silence. He wanted to forget. The last thing on his mind was love.

Elira was already a part of the town, almost like a myth—quiet, artistic, someone people noticed but didn't quite understand. She spent most days sitting on the last bench in the campus library, sketching clouds in her journal, watching storms come and go.

They met when they reached for the same book—Letters to the Moon. Their fingers brushed. He looked up. She smiled softly and said, "You can take it. I've already read it with my heart."

That moment was nothing.
And somehow, it was everything.

II. Friendship – A Quiet Kind of Magic

They started talking—about poetry, silence, grief, stars, and the beauty of things that didn't last. Their friendship wasn't loud. It didn't burst into the world. It grew like ivy—slow, unnoticed, but strong enough to climb stone.

Elira had a rule: no phones when they were together. "Presence," she'd say, "is the most beautiful form of love."

They walked through the woods, shared snacks on broken benches, and made up stories about strangers. They never spoke of love, but in the way Aarav untied her hair when she got tired, and in the way she carried his sorrows like her own—there was something holy in the silence...

III. Falling – Without Trying To

One night, as they lay on a rooftop beneath a sky bruised with stars, Elira whispered :

"Do you think people are meant to find just one person?" Aarav paused. "I think... we find the one who makes us feel found."

She turned her head and said, "Then I hope you never feel lost again."

That's when he kissed her—slow, trembling, and full of everything unsaid...

After that, everything changed... and nothing did.

They didn't start calling each other "boyfriend" or "girlfriend." They just became—more...

IV. Their Beautiful Days – The Golden Chapter

The months that followed felt like borrowed heaven.

They painted her bedroom ceiling with constellations.

They buried a time capsule under the willow tree where they had their first fight. They danced barefoot during storms, drank chai on foggy mornings, and took photos on film cameras that never got developed.

He'd write her letters and leave them in random books at the library. She'd write him songs on paper and tape them to his bedroom door.

"I love you" wasn't said often—but it was always there...

V. The Cracks – The Real World Creeps In

But even love wrapped in stars cannot escape gravity.

Aarav's mother fell ill back in his hometown. He had to travel often.

Elira's father lost his job and started drinking again. She stopped laughing as much.

They argued more. About time. About being enough. About the future neither of them could afford to plan.

Once, during a fight in the pouring rain, Elira screamed, "Why do I feel more alone with you than I ever did without you?"

Aarav didn't answer. He just stared, heart breaking, realizing even the sky they shared was changing.

But always—always—they came back to each other. Their love didn't fade. It just fought harder.

VI. The Storm No One Expected – The Beginning of the End

It started with Elira's fainting. Then the nosebleeds. Then the seizures.

The diagnosis : a terminal neurovascular disease. Rapid. Irreversible.

She smiled through it. Braver than death. But Aarav shattered.

"Run," she told him. "Live while you still can." He knelt before her and said, "Living is not living if it's not with you."

So they decided to live... what little they had left

VII. The Last Chapter – Love, Fully and Finally

They stopped everything else. No hospitals. No pity. Just them.

They moved to a small cottage near the lake where the clouds always looked like dreams.

Each day, they wrote one line of a poem. Each night, they kissed like it might be the last.

She faded slowly. Her laughter thinned. Her fingers shook. Her voice weakened. But her eyes—they still held fire.

On the last day, they lay side by side under the stars, wrapped in a shared blanket.

"I'm scared," she whispered. "Then let me hold your fear," he whispered back.

She closed her eyes.

When morning came, the sky was bluer than it had ever been.

Elira didn't wake. Aarav did. Just for a while...

VIII. The Final Goodbye

He buried her under the willow tree with the time capsule.

Inside it were the poems they wrote together.

On top, he carved into the bark : "Here lies the girl who taught the sky how to feel."

A month later, as the first snow fell, Aarav walked into the lake.

He didn't leave a note. Only her scarf. And a line written in water : "And now, I follow the only road that leads back to you."

The Story
They Left Behind

Years passed.

The cottage still stood.

Tourists still passed the lake,

wondering why it felt sacred.

One child once said she saw a boy and a girl

sitting by the willow, laughing.

And maybe... she did.

Because love like theirs doesn't disappear.

It becomes the wind.

The rain.

The silence before dawn.

And the sky?

It never forgot their names...

A Part of You Still Lives in Me

We're not together anymore,
but your birthday is still saved in my heart.
I still hear your voice in quiet moments, still
remember your scent like it never left.
Your photos... I never had the heart to delete them.
The nickname you gave me still makes me smile.
I still remember your number without trying.
And the truth is
I remember everything.
Every little detail.
Because even now,
a part of you, My Forever
You are the dawn that paints my skies...

In your arms, the world feels still,
A gentle warmth, a love so real.
The quiet bond that words can't say....
We speak through touch, and drift away.....
Your heartbeat soft against my chest.....
A rhythmic song, a welcome rest.
The world outside may rush and spin....
But here in your embrace, I win.
No need for promises or fears,
Just your love wiping away the years.....
In this simple, tender hold,
We find a story, yet untold.
In this hug, I feel our soul....
Two hearts that merge, that make us whole.....
A moment paused, a love soo true,
I find the universe in you....
It's enough for me for rest of a year....

A spark of light in love-lit eyes.

The whispered song the stars compose...

The softest touch my heartbeat knows...

You are the tide that pulls me near...

A voice so warm, so crystal clear.

Like moonlight draped in silver streams....

You dance within my sweetest dreams.

Your laughter sings, a melody,

That turns the world to poetry.

With every glance, my soul takes flight,

You are my day, my depth...

In a fleeting moment, her beauty did shine,
At she flipped her hair, a sight so divine.
For just a second, my heart skipped a beat,
Her elegance and grace, oh, what a treat.
Her hair in the breeze, like silk i did flow,
Abrief, stolen glance, my heart all aglow.
Though just a second, it felt like much more,
Her beauty lefi me longing, wanting for more.
So worth i, that moment, a memory to hold,
Her radiance, a treasure, more precious than gold.
In the blink of an eye, I found my delight,
Her beauty, a vision, a star in the night.

I know the silence lingers long,
A quiet where our laughter belonged...
Whispers roam, unkind, unfair,
And I feel lost without you there.
They speak of things we never knew...
Twisting words, distorting truth.
But in my heart, I've always known...
Our bond is built on love alone.
I miss the way we'd talk for hours,
The way we'd share our darkest hours...
I miss your smile, your caring so much...

I never told you, but I feel it deep,
A longing I bury, a secret I keep.
In every smile, in every glance,
I wish you'd see, I wish for a chance.
You're my laughter, my safety, my friend,
But sometimes I wonder, will this ever end?
I stand beside you, a silent prayer,
Hoping you'd notice, hoping you'd care.
When you talk of him, my heart does break,
But I smile, for your joy's at stake.
You'll never see the tears I hide,
The ache that comes when you're by his side.
It's not your fault, it's not your crime,
But I wonder, what if it was our time?
What if the bond we share could be more,
Than the friendship we're meant to adore?
But I'll stay quiet, keep this inside,
A love I carry, I cannot confide...

For your happiness means more to me,
Even if I'm the one who can't be free.
So here's to the moments, to what we've been,
To the love I feel, but can't let in.
I'll be your friend, always, you see,
Even if you'll never notice me...

In shadows deep, I walk alone,
A heart once bright, now turned to stone.
Each step a whisper, a quiet plea,
A soul that's lost, struggling to be free.
The laughter fades, the smiles grow thin,
As if the joy I knew was never in.
Beneath the weight of unspoken fears,
I carry the burden of forgotten years.
Dreams once vivid, now turned to dust,
In a world that's broken, I've lost my trust.
The skies above are painted gray,
And hope seems distant, far away.
I search for light in endless night,
Yet find no solace, no end in sight.
A river of tears, unseen, unfelt,
A silent ache no words can melt.
If only time could heal the pain,
Or grant me peace to break the chain.
But here I stand, lost in my strife,
A fading ghost in my own life.

Through Tears, I Love You...

A boy with wounds that never heal,
His heart, a storm that none can feel.
With every breath, a painful plea,
But still, it's you he longs to see.
His body frail, his spirit worn,
Through sleepless nights, through days of scorn,
Yet in the silence, deep and vast,
He loves you still, though shadows cast.
The doctors say there's little time,
A fleeting heart, a rhythm, rhyme,
But still, his soul beats only true—
A quiet vow: he'll wait for you.
His tears are rivers, flowing deep,
A pain so sharp, it makes him weep,
But in his eyes, you'll find no lies—
Just hope that never, ever dies.
Each day a battle, yet he stands,
With trembling heart and shaking hands,
Through broken bones and aching chest,
It's you, my love, who makes him rest...

We didn't fall apart all at once
it was slow.
Like leaves letting go of trees
when no one's watching.
We stopped saying "good morning"
with the same warmth.
We still said "I love you"...

Our smiles used to mean something,
now they're just habits—
ghosts on our faces
pretending not to ache.
I still remember the way
you used to reach for my hand
like it was your anchor—
and now
I am adrift in oceans
you no longer swim.
There were nights
I cried without sound,
hoping you'd feel it
from miles away.
And maybe you did...
but distance isn't just space,
sometimes it's silence
between two heart
that once beat the same...

A Promise Forever

From the moment I first saw your eyes,
I knew that love would paint the skies.
A spark, a glow, so pure and bright,
Guided me to you that fateful night.
Through laughter shared and tears we've dried,
You've stood beside me, heart open wide.
In every moment, big or small,
You've been my strength, my all in all.
With you, I've learned what love can mean,
In every word and every dream.
Now, as I stand before you here,
I promise to love you, year by year.
So, will you walk with me through time,
Together, in rhythm, your hand in mine?
With you, I know I'll always be,
Forever yours, and you, forever me.
Will you marry me, my love, my friend?
A journey together that will never end...